How Ya' Like My Hat?

There's a cover for every dome

- The 1st set of Hats -

For information address:

J2B Publishing LLC
4251 Columbia Park Road
Pomfret, MD 20675
www.J2BLLC.com
GladToDoIt@gmail.com

Printed and bound in the United States of America.

This book is set in Garamond.

ISBN: 978-1-954682-18-4

Visit Jim "The Houseboat Poet" McDonald at jfmcdonaldjr.com.

How Ya' Like My Hat?

There's a cover for every dome

- The 1st set of Hats –

Jim "The Houseboat Poet" McDonald

J2B Publishing

Also by
Jim "The Houseboat Poet" McDonald

Twilight to Son Shine
Life Changes
Ebb and Flow
Your 3-Words, My Little Story

Dedication

I dedicate this book to:

<u>(Insert your own name here)</u>

any and all of my readers that like being associated with my words.

If you feel someone is in danger of committing suicide,
you can contact the 'National Suicide Prevention Lifeline'
24 hours a day 7 days a week at:
1-800-273-8255

If you need help with any kind of addiction or mental illness,
you can contact the 'SAMHSA's National Helpline'
'Substance Abuse and Mental Health Services Administration'
24 hours a day 7 days a week at:
1-800-662-help (4357)

Acknowledgements

The adopted daughter of my heart, Maria Alvey, told her husband Bean, "Wow Jim is doing great. He is selling a lot of books." It was nice to hear her interest of anything that has to do with me. She lives deep in the center of my heart. Thank you, Sweetie.

My friend and publisher, Jim Brewster, often tells me, "Write more." I have wanted to write this book for years, so this is another dream come true. He is presently pushing me to add another category to my publications.

I would like to acknowledge my friends Raymond Davis and Wally Spooner for their constant encouragement for me to stick with my writing and studies at University of Maryland Global Campus (UMGC).

I have been known to tell a tall tale or two. The following stories are either fact, fiction, or a mix of both. Approximately half of them are fiction. I bought most of the hats from yard sales, thrift stores or flea markets, but some were given to me by friends for a *'How ya' like my hat?'* story. Which category do you feel each story falls in? The answers to your unrelenting inquiries are on the 'Fact or Fiction?' page at the back of the book.

Contents

Introduction

I've wanted to write stories for decades. When I became a disabled carpenter, I had time to devote to this passion; but would I? Then a question I read online challenged me with, "If you knew no one was going to read your work, would you still write it?" I thought about the question for days and concluded, "Of course I would!"

This book theme and the 'How ya' like my Hat?" stories stem from my trip to the Holy Land in Israel. In 1995 my ex-wife and I joined several members from our church on that trip. During the tour we stopped by a little bend in the Jordan River, which was exciting beyond measure. After watching a friend get baptized IN THE JORDAN RIVER, we stopped in a little market and bought an Australian looking hat, because the sun was beating on my fair skinned head. That hat is on the cover. The excitement to tell everyone about the trip, induced me to post a photo of me wearing the hat and a story about it. The title of the story was, *How ya' like my Hat?* That quickly became the category title of all my hat stories. Hope you enjoy my little teaser stories and photos.

I am not sure of the purchase dates, and below each photo is a general era of when the photo was taken. My brother's name was George and occasionally I use his name as a fictitious character in some of my stories. I apologize for the blurriness of some of the photos, can't go back in time yet to fix them. I know I could have just said sombrero instead of sombrero hat, but then it wouldn't have flowed like I wanted. Feel free to contact me with your thoughts.

Jordan River Hat

(Bought February 1995 in Israel, picture taken 2013)

I was in Israel in 1995. As I packed for the Ten-Day Holy Land Tour, I never thought about a hat to keep the sun off my head. There was sun and sand everywhere, Israel's color was tan with not much greenery. At some point our guide took us to a bend in a little river where a friend of mine got baptized. She was part of the larger group, but also one of the few from my church. I was already baptized, but I really wanted to do it again, because it was the Jordan River. Wow, the Jordan River, too cool.

I had a chance to ride a camel while I was there, but my pastor talked me out of it. He said they are filthy smelling animals and I would smell bad all day long. So I decided not to. I've regretted that decision ever since. I will probably never get a chance to ride a camel again.

Is this story fact, fiction, or a mix of both?

McDonald Hat - 1

(2019)

I went in one of my local McDonald's, because I had a hankering for their new Bacon Big Mac. After I ordered my meal, I noticed my server was wearing a new McDonald hat. I thought of my story category called, "*How ya' Like my Hat?*" and asked if I could speak with the manager. When the manager came over, I showed her my driver's license pointing to my last name – McDonald.

She said, "Oh?"

I told her, "I collect hats, especially McDonald hats." I then pointed to my server and asked, "Can I get one like that."

She replied, "Because of the M?"

"Yes."

"Let me see." She turned and went to the back of the store and returned with the hat I'm wearing in this photo.

"Thank you so much." I adjusted the band, put it on, grabbed my food, and walked out the door.

I immediately felt something was wrong in my universe, but I had food so the universe had to take a back seat. I pulled out of the parking lot and headed north toward the La Plata College of Southern Maryland (CSM) campus for my Thursday afternoon Communications course. I noticed a car full of people behind me wearing Burger King hats, but didn't think much of it till they got close and followed me down Mitchel Road toward the college.

I was a little concerned with my tailgater as I moved through the shady, crooked Mitchel Rd., then I saw another car full of people behind them and they were wearing Wendy's hats. At this point, my food took a back seat to the immediate threat of the hat brigade.

Luck has a way of finding me when I need it the most and as I was pulling into one of the campus parking lots, I saw a large crowd of people. Everyone in this crowd was wearing CSM hats – there were hundreds of my fellow Hawks (students) coming to my rescue. Somehow the universe let my friends know I was in trouble. When the Burger King and Wendy's people saw this, they turned and slipped quietly off the college grounds.

Is this story fact, fiction, or a mix of both?

Fuzz Ball Hat

(2018)

I was enjoying my normal Sunday morning at the White Plains Flea Market, when I came across this fuzz ball hat. I had no desire to buy it, but I did want some pictures for my *How ya' like my hat?* gig.

I asked the vendor, Reggie, "Can you take some pictures of me wearing this hat?"

He said, "Sure."

I took off my Washington Redskin hat and posed for some pictures, figuring six photos were enough to choose from. I said, "Thank you." as I sat the hat back in its place.

Reggie said, “You can have it for a buck.”

I, “stuttered” for a moment.

Then he said, “Just take it, it’s yours.”

I gave him a dollar. Then I put the hat back on my head, said, “Thank you,” and headed further into the market.

A friend of mine stared at my funny hat and said, “That hat’s much better, than the one in your hand.” He was a Dallas Cowboy fan and wearing a Cowboy hat.

I sent him a sideways grin while saying, “Yeah, yeah, yeah, I’ll give you a dollar for your hat.”

“You have two already. What do you want with mine?”

“I have to use the rest room and there is no toilet paper.”

“Get out of here you fool,” he shot back. We hugged and went our separate ways.

Later at the La Plata, Starbucks, my barista stared at my fuzz ball hat.

“Nice hat.”

“You want it?”

“How much?”

“Nothing, it’s yours.”

Is this story fact, fiction, or a mix of both?

Lincoln Hat

(2007)

Not too long ago I got a terrible sunburn on my head. It was so bad, that it blinded me whenever I looked in the mirror.

I normally always wear a hat, but during my move to Virginia, I lost several boxes off of my truck. One box had my socks and underwear, another one had shoes and pants, a third had most of my t-shirts, and the last one had all of my hats.

I took a break from unpacking after I noticed the boxes missing, and went to a local store. I bought underwear, socks, t-shirts, and pants. However, I was not going to spend ten dollars for a hat I wasn't interested in.

It was a hot, windy, Saturday and not good for outdoor shopping without a hat, but I went anyway. There were plenty of yard sales in this sleepy little town, but I didn't find the flea market until hours later. Finally came across a table with a large assortment of hats, I must have spent twenty minutes trying on one after another. Finding a few Washington Redskin hats, for a buck apiece was a prize in itself. Temporarily setting them aside, I kept searching for fun. While trying on an Abraham Lincoln hat, a big gust of wind blew it off my head. Before I could react, a dog caught it and quickly ran off. I didn't want it anyway, because it was too small to fit my noggin and it cost ten dollars.

The lady said, "That will be ten dollars, please."

I said, "That wasn't my fault."

"You tried on almost every hat and got your head sweat on every one of them."

Not knowing what to do, I said, "Okay" and gave her twelve dollars for the Lincoln and two Redskin's hats.

Later that evening, as I was rubbing Aloe Vera on my sun burned head, there was a knock on my front door. It was the hat lady and she was carrying a fruit basket. She handed me the basket and said, "I have something else for you."

While taking the fruit basket, I said, "WOW! Wasn't expecting this."

She turned to her truck and "whistled." A dog jumped out of truck bed and sprinted to her side. She said, "Want you to meet Darby."

Darby sat by her side with a bag hanging from his bottom jaw. I realized Darby was the same dog that grabbed the Lincoln hat and ran off.

"Think he likes you and was playing with you earlier, not sure though." She took the bag from Darby, then handed it and ten dollars to me, and said, "Welcome to the neighborhood."

Is this story fact, fiction, or a mix of both?

Lowes Hat

(2007)

(2017)

I was shopping in Lowes while wearing my Home Depot hat that I got in North Carolina. When I asked for help, I received mixed replies. One employee said with a grin, "We don't serve your kind."

Another pointed to the exit and said, "Everything you need is right through that door." Then a third employee offered to trade me three brand new Lowe's buckets for my hat.

Three buckets were set on my load of wood, while he said, "If you want these buckets, all you have to do is throw that hat in the trash." He said that while pointing to a trash can next to the contractor's counter.

I took it off and replied, "What would I wear outside as a melanoma hat? Do you have a Lowes hat for my *How ya' like my hat* gig?"

"What do you mean *How ya' like my hat* gig?"

"It's a little thing I do. I buy used hats, have someone take photos of me wearing them, then write a story about the hat. Next, I post a photo and the corresponding story on Facebook. Some of the stories are fact and some are fiction."

"Let me see if I can find you a hat."

He came back with two different Lowes hats to choose from. I chose this one and made a deal not to wear the Home Depot hat in Lowes anymore.

Is this story fact, fiction, or a mix of both?

Burger King Hat

(2012)

I followed her out of the lounge, through the city streets and into the park, wishing I had a camera.

I sat on the bench behind her, as she stood watching hundreds of ducks in and around the pond. She sat on the left side of a bench and started feeding the ducks.

She was wearing an ugly paper Burger King hat that didn't come close to matching the rest of her attire. When I finally took the plunge, I stood and awkwardly walked to her right and said, "You look nice today." Then asked, "May I join you?"

At that moment, sirens from what seemed to be a police chase, echoed off the pond and through the trees and bushes. Instead of answering me she said, "Duck!"

I replied, "Why? I'm not wanted by the police."

"No. I mean duck." She pointed to a baby duck at my feet.

"Oh wow! I never noticed; I was too busy looking at your hat."

"Only my hat?"

"Well, now that you ask…"

"Yeah, I lost a bet to a guy that works at Wendy's. We all make fun of this stupid hat."

"What was the bet?"

"I bet him that he would fail his English test. He passed, so I had to walk to the park in a bikini of his choosing, high heels, and this hat."

"Must say, he has a nice eye for fashion." Then I asked, "Can I get a picture?"

"Of me in my bikini?"

"No, of me in that hat. Can you take a picture of me wearing it?"

She seemed stunned, but said, "Sure."

Is this story fact, fiction, or a mix of both?

McDonald Hat - 2

(2014)

In 1972, McDonald's hired a crew of sixteen-year-old misfits and hooligans to run closing shift for their brand-new store in Waldorf, MD. I was one of them; a young boy and a good student until I joined that crew. My friend there gave me my first full beer and first joint, and my life began its downhill slide from which I did not recover until I met Jesus at age 35. What happened to me is not McDonald's fault and our crew, while a bit wild, did our jobs, made McDonald's money, and still had fun.

We were the late shift and had two shift managers that weren't much older than us whom we enjoyed working with, but we couldn't find anything good to say about the store manager. Add to that the fact that the last thing on our minds after closing up for the night was not sleep and you have the ingredients for trouble.

One night we got a hold of some self-adhesive stickers like you can get in a bubble gum machine. Then one of us had the bright idea to go back to our McDonalds and use the stickers to write a slogan on the outside of the walk-in freezer in the parking lot. I was in the driver's seat when we parked next to the freezer, so it was my job to place the stickers it. The others were opening the small plastic containers holding the stickers and throwing the containers out the window onto the parking lot. I was spelling a word expressing our displeasure with our store manager. I had completed the first letter, "F" and was starting on the "U" when we heard the sound of plastic containers being crushed under tires. It was a state police officer. He was on our passenger side. He asked, "What are you guys up to?"

Luckily, we were still in our work uniforms and wearing our silly paper McDonalds hats so he could see we had a reason to be there. While the officer was busy taking our information, I reached out my window and quickly wiped the stickers off the ice box. He left shortly after that, leaving us giggling and sweating.

Is this story fact, fiction, or a mix of both?

Silly Hat

(2016)

I was in line at WAWA, when I noticed a very attractive lady in line ahead of me. I studied her outfit for a second or two, which looked like an exercise outfit. I then told her, "I'll let you pay for my gas, if you let me take a picture of you."

She answered my comment with a hardy laugh and a resounding, "NO!" then laughed some more.

I am, so glad when people get my, sometimes stupid, humor and it feels so good to hear them laugh. I replied, "Ok. I'll pay for my gas and take a picture of you."

"Ok, but you have to let me take a picture of you wearing that silly hat."

Of course I said, "Deal!" thinking solely of my *How ya' like my hat?* gig.

Here is the picture she took.

Is this story fact, fiction, or a mix of both?

Graduation Hat

(2016)

A friend brought this to me and said, "Bet you won't wear this one."

I put it on my head and said, *"How ya' like my hat?"*

He said, "You look stupid."

"What else is new?"

"What kind of story will you write about it?"

I said, "Nothing. I'll put it on my head, take a picture of it, post it, and then ask, *'How ya' like my hat?'*"

"You have to write a story."

"No I don't, watch."

Is this story fact, fiction, or a mix of both?

Flag Hat

(2016)

I was visiting Washington D.C., when I saw a small demonstration in the middle of the street. It caught my eye because it was colorful and loud. There were only a few dozen people, but still enough to block the road.

Even though I know DC very well, the notion of turning around irritated me. Especially, since these people were keeping me from my appointment for their personal gain.

I parked fifty feet away, then walked to a vendor that was selling Americana paraphernalia. I bought a hat, flag, and some water.

I had no problem sneaking into the small crowd and when I was in the middle of it, I put the hat on and raised my flag high yelling, "Hey! Hey! USA!"

I noticed my actions were causing problems for the demonstrators because they started shouldering up to me and were trying to nudge me out.

Some by-standers noticed this, so they went to the same vendor, bought some hats and flags, and joined my chant. "Hey! Hey! USA!" We yelled this over and over and even more people joined me in the chant. Soon we outnumbered the picketers.

It was quite funny because some of the original demonstrators started chanting with us. Since we now outnumbered the demonstrators, we started nudging them out.

Before we knew it, we were the only one's chanting. Then the crowd slowly dissipated until I was the only one there. I felt a little stupid standing in the middle of the street all by myself, so I left.

Is this story fact, fiction, or a mix of both?

Tennessee Hat

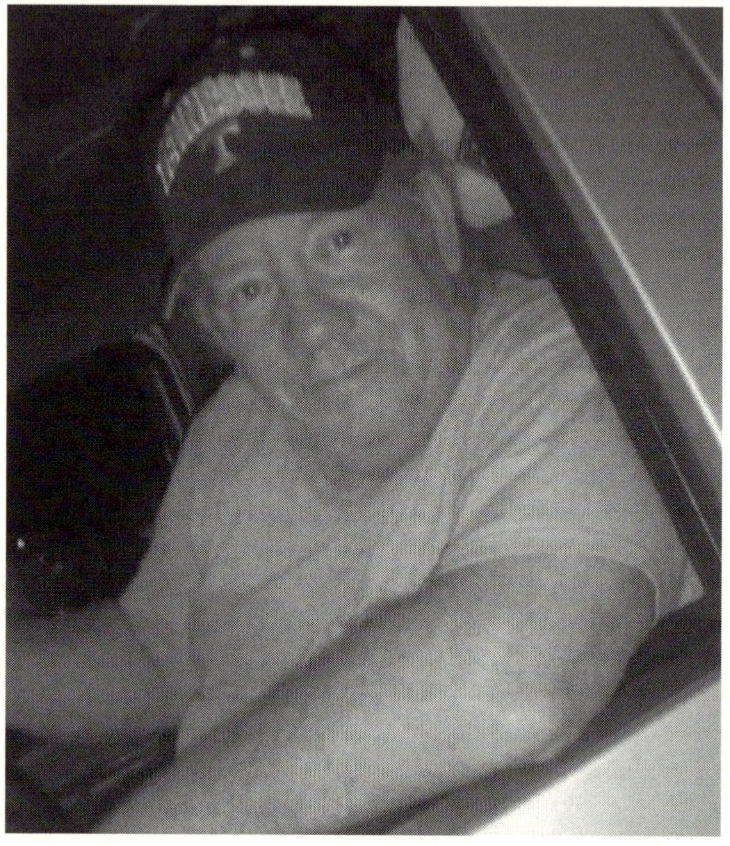

(2012)

I'm from the DMV, also known as the District of Columbia, Maryland, and Virginia. I was born in Fort Belvoir, Virginia, worked many years in DC, and lived most of my life in Maryland, so I am DMV all over.

Dad's family is from Sulfur Springs, Texas. In my childhood I visited there twice. It took Dad and I twenty-two hours of nonstop driving, to arrive at the family house in 1972. It is halfway across the country and we did not have the cash or time to visit more often.

Mom's family is from Mountain City, Tennessee. It only took eight hours to get there, now with better roads I can make it in six hours.

Dad probably went to Mountain City only a half a dozen times, so normally mom took us kids. Our stays typically lasted two weeks and that was every summer. Needless to say, I became very attached to Mountain City.

I have a whole mess of family buried down there, but still have at least six first cousins and their offspring living there.

I came across three hats with the Tennessee Volunteer colors and the big "T" on them in North Carolina. I paid a dollar apiece. I'm going to keep this one, so if any of my cousins wants one of the other two, let me know.

Little Hat

(2007)

Raymond and I were at a thrift store in North Carolina, where I found twenty or so hats for cheap.

I was trying some on, when one of the salesmen walked over and asked, "What kind of hat are you looking for?"

I told him, "I have this bit, on Facebook, called *How ya' like my hat?* and I often look for Washington Redskin hats, but sometimes I come across a hat that speaks to me and says, 'write about me.' "

He picked up this little one and asked, "What does this one say to you?"

"It says, 'I have a big head.' "

"Well, it doesn't fit very well, that's for sure." We both laughed at his little joke. "But it is funny looking. Think of the story you can write about it!"

Afterwards I took the hat up to the cash register, but had no idea what kind of story I was going to write. However, as I was walking away from the counter, I heard him tell the girl who took my money, "Did you see the stupid little hat I sold to the Redskin fan? I told you I could sell it."

She said, "If he only knew you were a Dallas Cowboy fan."

Is this story fact, fiction, or a mix of both?

Jesus Hat

(2016)

Jesus most certainly is my Boss!

Some hats I buy because I like the sport team. Some because they're funny, interesting, or simply I like what's written on them. This one is the latter.

My boss is Jesus! In 1990, I made a decision that affected my whole life. It was when I accepted Jesus Christ as my personal Savoir. I am not perfect by any stretch of the imagination, but I am a much better person now that Jesus is in my life.

I lost my home several years ago and now space is limited. This means I have little room to store or keep things. After I buy a hat, take a picture of it, I then try to find a nice home for it. This nice-looking head covering was sitting in my van for weeks, when I came across an old friend walking the neighborhood. I put my van in park and we talked of old and new times. I have always felt this is how people should visit, right when the time presents itself. She was leaning on the van, telling me about the conversation she was just having with God, while shading her eyes from the sun. It was so nice to see how enthusiastic she was about God. I peacefully listened in silence.

God often presents me with little signs, reminding me of His presence. This one was perfect. I reached into the back seat to get my friend Debbie, her new hat and I sat quietly in my seat as I handed her this gift from God. It was a flawless moment in time, that I shared with Debbie and most importantly we shared it with God.

Is this story fact, fiction, or a mix of both?

Forest Park Baptist Church Hat

(1995)

This is not a very good view of the hat, but I like the action photo of me playing slow pitch softball. Well, except for that big belly. Our team was "Forest Park Baptist Church" and it was part of the "Southern Maryland All Faith League." Lots of fun to be had all around, winning or losing.

I can tell that I was the coach that year, because of the color of the hat and jersey. They used to be light blue, but I thought green would fit the name, Forest, better. So we took a vote and changed the color.

Considering the direction everyone is looking, I must have hit the ball towards left field. I wouldn't be surprised if it was a dribbler to third.

During my tenure at the church, I played every position except pitcher, first, left field, and center field. I normally played third all my life, but by this time of my life my best position was second. I still had a good glove, but my arm was old.

One year when we were still in the blue jerseys, God used me to schedule and play a game against the local "Southern Maryland Pre-Release Unit" inmates. I used to deliver the Gospel message there for several years, till there was an incident. The state shut down all incoming volunteer outreaches to that facility. Nothing we did and the game was before that happened.

Some of the guys were apprehensive about going into the institution, but again we took a vote and everyone on our team stepped up and played for Jesus. There was no sermon, no preaching, just a good ole American Pastime. Can't remember who won, but it was a great game and day.

It was not this game, but I do remember hitting one to short and the fighter in me wanted to run it out. My mind and the top part of my body were going faster than the bottom part of my body, so halfway to first I fell flat on my face. I gave the safe sign, which got a good laugh from everyone. Thank God there was no camera that day.

Is this story fact, fiction, or a mix of both?

Skin's Hat

(2009)

I was sweating so much, that I was afraid to put my hands on their hips.

As you can see this hat attracts women and I knew it hypnotically charmed the ladies, so I wore it everywhere.

A couple of years ago, I was enjoying one of my favorite joys in life, yard-sailing, when a lady kept getting closer and closer to me. She gently rubbed her right side against my left side and of course, I was enjoying every minute of this little interlude. However, her boyfriend wasn't and he made his objections known when he yelled, "WHAT'S GOING ON HERE?"

I turned while shrugging my shoulders, especially when I saw how big he was. A huge young man and I wanted no part of their little games. I tried to say something, but thought better of it.

I knew how to fix the problem though. I simply took off the hat. The young lady all of sudden moved to her left and looked at me with disgust, while saying to her boyfriend, "What?"

I shrugged my shoulders and looked at her in dismay. When they started arguing, I slipped away to safety, to my right, and never looked back.

Some people in section 454 were calling me the Tie Guy.

Is this story fact, fiction, or a mix of both?

Camouflage Hat

(2016)

I can't remember where or when I got this hat, but I'm sure I didn't pay much for it. Raymond took this picture, while I was kneeling behind Mom and Dad's tombstone at Arlington National Cemetery.

In 2007, Raymond and I were in North Carolina eating breakfast, when he asked our waitress, "Anything fun to do around here?"

She said, "No, you're in Murphy, North Carolina! Oh, there is a rodeo tonight." Then she gave us the information we needed to get there.

Raymond asked, "Are you going?"

"Maybe, I'm not sure yet."

"Hope to see you there."

We went to the rodeo, because neither of us had ever been to one. We sat at the top of the bleachers near the middle of the arena. I was wearing this hat and one of the rodeo entertainers was wearing a huge red cowboy hat. I mean it was huge. The Big Red Hat guy said, "I want everyone to applaud when I call out the state you're from." He yelled out, "North Carolina!" Most of the spectators applauded, hooted, and hollered. He said, "Georgia!" Some of the crowd clapped. "How about Tennessee?" A few Tennesseans were there. Then he asked, "Did I miss anyone?"

I raised my hand and yelled, "Yes, me!"

He asked, "Where you from?"

"Maryland!" Raymond knows me very well, so as to not be embarrassed by me or connected to me he moved a couple spaces away from me to my right.

"What are you doing here?" replied the Big Red Hat guy.

"I'm talking to a guy with a big ugly red hat!"

He said, "You have no room to talk with that hat. Where did you get it?"

By this time Raymond was on the other side of the bench when I said, "I got it at Wal-Mart, next to an ugly big red hat."

The conversation went on for a few more minutes, then I guess Big Red Hat guy's time was up, because he waved at me and finished his segment. Our waitress was sitting in our section, in the front row. She stood and waved at us. I thought, that was cool. Raymond might not have got a wave if it wasn't for my loudmouth and outgoing nature.

Is this story fact, fiction, or a mix of both?

Mack in the Hat

(2013)

do not like
my silly hat
called Mack in
my silly hat
cheaply bought
my silly hat
green and white is
my silly hat
Mack in the hat with
my silly hat
tall and awkward is
my silly hat
little too tight is
my silly hat
I did not want
my silly hat
giveth away
my silly hat

Is this story fact, fiction, or a mix of both?

Flowerpot Hat

(2007)

Raymond and I were rambling around on a wooded back road in North Carolina with no particular destination, when we came across a little thrift shore on the left in the middle of nowhere. Since we love these types of stores, we turned around at the nearest driveway to go back to it.

When we pulled into the gravel parking lot, we laughed when we noticed a sign that said, "Treasures in the Middle of Nowhere." As we walked up the steps and through the French Doors, an elderly lady said, "How y'all doing?"

I said, "Fair to middling I reckon." I heard dad say that all the time.

Raymond said with a chuckle, "No he's not! He's never fair."

This was the only hat in the cute little shop; however, she wanted way too much for it. I tried it on and Raymond took a picture of me wearing the hat. The lady asked me, "Why are you wearing a flowerpot on your head?"

"What?"

"That's a flowerpot. The plastic insert is on the middle shelf behind you."

"I had no idea," I replied with a smile."

Raymond said, "Thought you knew it was flowerpot and you were just playing."

"No! Well, don't tell anyone. People might think I'm stupid."

Raymond looked at me and smiled, "Your friends already know that."

Tall Hat

(2014)

I was meeting some friends, when one of them pulled me off to the side and told me, "I'll give you a dollar, if you wear this hat during the whole meeting and lunch afterward."

I said, "No, but I'll do it for six."

"Why six?"

"That way I'll have money for lunch."

He said, "Okay," thinking he got me to do something that I normally wouldn't do.

After lunch, my friend George asked me, "Where did you get money for lunch?" I told him the deal I made and he said, "That's a pretty good deal for you."

"Yeah, it is." George knows I would have bought the hat for my *How ya' like my hat?* gig. This way I got the picture, story, and lunch for free.

Is this story fact, fiction, or a mix of both?

College of Southern Maryland Hat

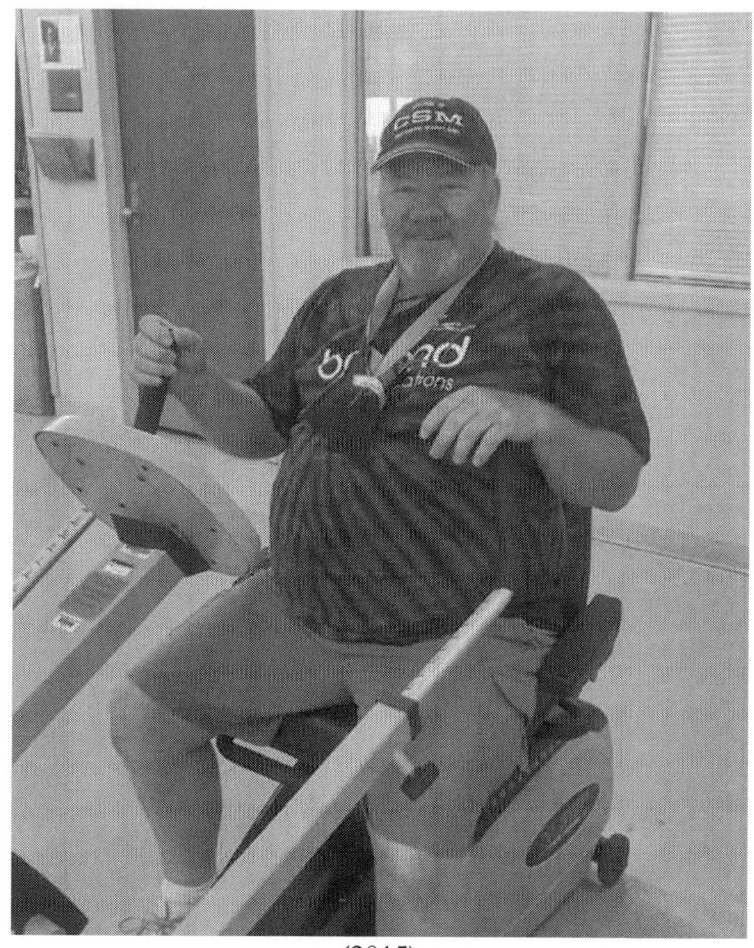

(2015)

I quit drinking and drugging in 1989. I was a freshly sober, single father with little direction. A few years later the government helped me go to college at Charles County Community College (CCCC), before it was known as College of Southern Maryland (CSM). At that time, I wanted to learn cyber security, but it was not offered. That left me still wanting something in the computer field, so Computer Science became my major.

Two years later, while still raising my sons, money became more of need, so I went back to carpentry.

In 2014, I became disabled and couldn't work in my field of carpentry, so I went back to school. This time as an English major. The road has been long and often very difficult for this old feeble mind. I love being able to say I stuck with it and received two Associate of Arts Degrees at CSM and working on my Bachelor's in English at University of Maryland Global Campus (UMGC). With encouragement from professors, family, and friends this will be my fourth published book.

This photo of me wearing my CSM hat was taken at University of Maryland Charles Regional Medical Center. I was there due to several different medical issues – COPD, type 2 diabetes, and now congestive heart failure to name the more prevalent issues.

I am here to say you can teach an old dog new tricks!

McDonald Hat - 3

(2016)

I was walking westward on route 6 in La Plata, MD., when a friend called me over and asked, "Hey Jim. Did you hear?"

I said, "Hear what?"

"People all over the county are talking about you."

"Oh no, that can't be good. Why, what's up?"

"Perhaps it's not a problem if you are a fan of McDonalds like you are." He then explained what was going on, "You wrote a story for the local paper about how all the meat for the local fast-food joints in Charles County, except for McDonald's, come from a pig farm in Nanjemoy."

"That's too funny. Guess they didn't read the last line of the story."

"Remind me what that line is."

"This story could be fact, fiction, or a mix of both. What category do you think it falls in?"

Is this story fact, fiction, or a mix of both?

Sombrero Hat

(2016)

I finally made it to the motel after a three-hour hiatus, caused by not one, but two flat tires.

Even though the road was lined on both sides by a mix of pine, spruce, maple, and oak trees, the sun still found its way to my bald spot. It was a scorching, blistering and unrelenting heat and I had no protection for my head.

Not only was the sun playing havoc on my head, but I also only had one spare and I already put it on the right rear and moved to the front. I was in the process of taking the right front tire off, when I noticed a guy standing over me blocking the sun. I said, "Thank God."

"No. I'm Steve," the guy said with a grin.

"Thank you for blocking the sun. Do you have a 275/60R15 tire on ya'?"

He felt his chest, his front pockets, then his back pockets and said, "No, but I do have a hat for that burnt spot on your head."

"I'll take it. Can I get a ride to the nearest service station?"

"Sure." We put both flats in the back of his truck and off we went.

Is this story fact, fiction, or a mix of both?

Hooters Hat

(2016)

Upset wasn't a strong enough word after reading the sign on the front door of Hooters. It read, "We are temporarily out of wings." The only reason we went there, was because of their World-Famous Wings.

You're probably thinking, yeah right, "You go there for the scantily clad women not the wings."

My girl fought me six ways to Sunday about even going there for lunch. She mentioned, "You only want to go for the short shorts and the bountiful cleavage." Well, she was right and it was a lot of work convincing her otherwise.

I told her, "I really have a taste for spicy wings and they have the best in town." I was faced with a dilemma I couldn't rectify. How could we still walk in and eat something else? My only recourse, was to turn to her and say, "Let's go to Jack's and get a burger."

She said with a devious grin, "Hooters also has good burgers. Let's go in."

We walked in, but I had a sinking feeling this was a trick!

Oriole's Hat

(2016)

My self and some friends went to Camden Yards to watch our O's beat the Yankees. That was our hope anyway. I had no desire to be around all those NY fans if they won. For years they would come down to our house and chant, "Let's go Yankees." That upset me to no end.

The first 25,000 fans got a free checkered floppy hat. It was a crappy looking hat, but well-made and it was an Orioles' hat. We got there late, so when a number of us were walking down South Paca St. we were worried we would not get a hat. We met the rest of our "Baltimore Orioles Insanity" group at the ticket office on the back side of the warehouse.

We were all together at the West Camden St. entrance, when we saw a small herd of Yankee fans getting our hats and stomping on them. Some of them were even lighting the hats on fire. We had a group of twenty, they had forty or so. The numbers didn't warn off James, Jimmy, Matt, Jason, or Brandon. I'm from the sixties, peace not war, so I was hanging back. When Brandon was heading into the fray, he turned to me and said, "You comin' old man?" I checked my crotch and noticed I did have a pair, so I followed him into the fracas. As we took on the Yanks, other bird fans, that we didn't know, joined in and it wasn't long before we had the numbers. The Yanks ran, we won, and that's how I got this hat.

Is this story fact, fiction, or a mix of both?

Cowgirl Hat

(2019)

One of my passions is going to yard sales, thrift stores and flea markets, but years ago I moved into a smaller home, which means most of my shopping at yard sales is strictly for fun – not for need or want. It's also good quality time if I'm with a family member or friend.

Typically what you do at yard sales, is casually pick an item up and ask, how much. If it's $1, I'll probably get it, otherwise I wouldn't have picked it up in the first place. If they say $5, I will normally put it down and move on, while not looking at them.

George and I were drifting through yard sales all morning long and hadn't found anything of value yet. Then I saw it, I knew I wanted a picture of me wearing it. I could tell from a distance that it was in ratty shape and figured it would be cheap. I was inching towards the hat, when I noticed a lady at the other end of the tables doing the same. Somehow, I knew she wanted it too. At first, we were the same distance from the hat, so I started to move a little quicker than normal. She moved quicker though and was within yards of it, but I was closer to the lady collecting the money, so I asked, "How much for the hat?"

The proprietor said, "Two dollars."

I said, "Sold." And quickly handed her the money, then reached over grabbed the hat and put it on my head.

I didn't know there was such a thing as a Cowgirl Hat, till the lady shopper told me, "You know that hat is for a girl, right?"

I said, "No way! What makes it a girl's hat?"

She said, "Let me show you." She reached for it, while it was still on my head.

"No way!" I grabbed it by the sides, pulling it down tight and curled it up even more than it already was.

She said, "Three, four, okay five dollars, and that's it!" She said all this, while my friend George took some pictures of me wearing the hat.

From the yard sale, we went to the Charlotte Hall Veterans Home, where I had some photos hanging in an art show. She followed us and while George and I were in the hallway looking at the photos, she walked around the corner and offered me ten dollars. I realized all I really wanted was some photos of the hat for this story, so I told her, "Here it's yours for free, if you take some pictures of me wearing it next to my photos hanging on this wall."

She said, "Great, which ones are yours?" She took several shots of me standing next to my photography, then we started talking about them.

During that time, I told her, "I buy hats for cheap, then write stories about them."

"What do you do with the hats after?"

"I normally give them to someone who wants them, like you. It worked out perfectly because I especially wanted these pictures with this hat."

I gave her my card, just before she sauntered down the hallway and out the door, then she stuck her head back in and said, "I'll take all the hats that you don't want. I'll even meet you and take the photos for your stories."

"Okay, call me."

Well we ended up dating, married, and divorced. It's so sad, because now she doesn't chase me anymore.

Is this story fact, fiction, or a mix of both?

Fact or Fiction?

Jordan River Hat.. 100% fact
McDonald Hat - 1....buying the hat was true, 75% fiction
Fuzz Ball Hat .... 100% fact
Lincoln Hat .... 100% fiction
Lowes Hat.. 100% fact
Burger King Hat... 100% fiction
McDonald Hat - 2.. 100% fact
Silly Hat.................... she did not take the photo, 90% fact
Graduation Hat.......................I did write a story, 80% fact
Flag Hat... 100% fiction
Tennessee Hat.. 100% fact
Little Hat........... did not hear them say anything, 85% fact
Jesus Hat .... 100% fact
Forest Park Baptist Church Hat .... 100% fact
Skin's Hat...................hands and tie guy are true, 85% fact
Camouflage Hat.. 100% fact
Mack in the Hat....................Mack is in the past, 90% fact
Flowerpot Hat... 100% fact
Tall Hat .... 100% fiction
College of Southern Maryland Hat .... 100% fact
McDonald Hat - 3.. 100% fiction
Sombrero Hat .... 100% fiction
Hooters Hat ....I like wings & scantily glad, 80% fiction
Oriole's Hat.. 100% fiction
Cowgirl HatI did have photography hanging,_80% fiction

The Houseboat Poet

Jim "The Houseboat Poet" McDonald, a Southern Maryland resident since 1965, was raised on a tobacco farm in Hughesville, MD. He hated it then, but would give his eyeteeth for it now. He planned to not be like his alcoholic father, but a high school marriage, two boys, sex, drinking, drugs, and three wives ended in his release from jail at age 35 and trying to recover his soul and his maturity. His constant source of love and affection through all this was his mother.

In 1989, while living in the Charles County Detention Center, he turned towards Jesus and away from the drink and drugs that had characterized his life for seventeen years. It was while he lived on a houseboat at the water's edge, feeling the tide come in and go out that he began to fulfill a life-long dream to write and be a poet, a dream he started in 2014.

Website -JF McDonald https://jfmcdonaldjr.com

Amazon author page https://amazon.com/author/jimmcdonaldjr

FB Jim McDonald Writes https://facebook.com/poetryandmorewords

FB personal https://www.facebook.com/jimmcdonaldjr

LinkedIn https://www.linkedin.com/in/jim-mcdonald-8119b256/

Instagram https://www.instagram.com/jfm_creates/

Twitter https://twitter.com/JFM_Creates/

Made in the USA
Middletown, DE
22 May 2022